Grades 4 up

SCOOP AFTER SCOOP

A HISTORY OF

by
Stephen Krensky

Illustrations by
Richard Rosenblum

CE CREAM

Atheneum
New York
1986

Atheneum
Macmillan Publishing Company
866 Third Avenue, New York, NY 10022

Type set by Fisher Composition, New York City
Printed and bound by Fairfield Graphics, Fairfield, Pennsylvania
Designed by Mary Ahern

10 9 8 7 6 5 4 3 2 1

Library of Congress Cataloging-in-Publication Data
Krensky, Stephen.   Scoop after scoop.

SUMMARY: A history of ice cream, from 4000 years ago
when the Egyptians mixed honey with crushed ice,
to the present day, in which 800 million gallons of ice cream
are consumed annually in the U.S. alone.
1. Ice cream, ices, etc.—Juvenile literature.
[1. Ice Cream, ices, etc.]   I. Rosenblum, Richard, ill.
II. Title.
TX795.K74   1986   641.8'62   86-3597
ISBN 0-689-31276-8

For my family

SCOOP AFTER SCOOP

THERE WAS A TIME BEFORE ICE CREAM, a time when nobody had ever heard of chocolate chip and butter pecan, but there was never a time before dessert. Even in prehistoric days, before alphabets and cities and music videos, everybody had a sweet tooth. The problem was, nobody could pay much attention to it. Everyone was too busy discovering fire and inventing the wheel. So people settled for snatching a few berries or stealing honey from unsuspecting bees.

In those days everyone was always on the move. When the food ran out in one place, people packed up their arrowheads and went somewhere else. Eventually they began to settle down, and with the time they saved from all that packing and unpacking, people made their desserts a little more complicated. Four thousand years ago, the ancient Egyptians were building pyramids by day and mixing honey with crushed fruit at night. In the following centuries, Hebrews, Greeks, and Persians made cakes and drinks with crushed fruit.

Some of these drinks were cold. The idea of cooling wine or juice on purpose was controversial at first. Some people thought cold drinks were dangerous, that they were a great shock to the body. Other people disagreed. They thought the drinks were more refreshing when chilled. Fortunately for ice cream, the second group won out.

But just because they enjoyed cold drinks did not mean these ancient people could have them whenever they wanted. The drinks were cooled in snow or ice, neither of which was sitting around the front door in the warm Mediterranean climate. They had to be carried down from the mountains. Most people did not have the extra time to fetch snow or ice for themselves, and hiring someone else to fetch it was expensive. Only rich people could afford to do that.

There were a lot of rich people in Rome. The city had been founded in 783 B.C., and the Romans spent most of the next eight centuries conquering much of Europe, North Africa, and the Middle East. A lot of them became wealthy in the process. They lived in large houses, they sat on handsomely carved chairs, and they ate off gold dishes decorated with jewels.

Rich Romans with fancy plates naturally wanted a fancy meal to go on the plates. They often hosted elaborate banquets featuring foods from all parts of their empire. And the Romans weren't shy about what they ate. They would try almost anything, from flamingo tongues to fish livers.

For the Roman emperors, such meals were common. After all, they were in charge and had to set an example. One of them, Nero Claudius Caesar, set many examples. Most of them were bad. He was seventeen when he became emperor in A.D. 54. Nero did some governing here and there, but his main concern was having fun. Nero loved to eat and some of his meals went on for days without stopping.

One of his special treats at these banquets required careful planning. He would order some slaves to run to the mountains and gather some snow. The snow was then carried to Nero's table.

There it was mixed with fruit juices, honey, or wine. The resulting sweet ices were served to the emperor and his guests.

These sweet ices were the first frozen desserts we know of. Nero might have made other dessert advances had he only lived longer. But his unpopular ruling habits caught up with him. Nero was a ruthless man (he had ordered his mother and wife killed when they threatened his position), and ruthless men make enemies. Nero made so many that he took his own life at age thirty-one before his enemies got the chance.

The Western Roman Empire lasted another 400 years, but frozen desserts made no further progress. The different emperors apparently had other things on their minds. When the northern armies of Huns and Visigoths finally overran Rome in 486, progress of all kinds was halted. These invaders had no time for science and literature, and no taste for fancy banquets. They simply destroyed Rome and carried off its treasures. The Romans who survived forgot about sweet ices.

The end of the Western Roman Empire plunged Europe into the Dark Ages. The halt in trade and the decline of knowledge made life more difficult. Food was harder to come by, and people took what they could get. They ate coarse bread and heavily salted meat; they drank warm beer and wine. Desserts, even simple ones like fruits and nuts in pastry shells, were few and far between.

The Crusades finally helped to wake up the European taste buds. This series of religious wars was fought during the eleventh, twelfth, and thirteenth centuries in the Middle East. The European soldiers who took part made many adjustments—to a different climate, to unfamiliar customs, and to strange foods. Whatever they thought of the climate and customs, a lot of the soldiers enjoyed their meals. When they returned home, they brought a taste for new things, like oranges and pepper, back with them.

Many Crusaders were carried across the Mediterranean in ships from Venice. This Italian city, surrounded by water and crisscrossed by canals, was an independent naval power. It had become a center of trade—a place where silk, gold, and spices from the East were exchanged for honey, wool, and furs from the West.

Venice was a stopping place for many travelers, some of whom had explored the extent of the known world. The most famous of them was a Venetian himself. Marco Polo was only seventeen years old when he first left home. He departed from Venice in 1271 with his father and uncle on a trip to China. Their journey took the Polos through the Middle East, Persia, China, Singapore, and India. It covered 15,000 miles (24,000 kilometers) and took twenty-four years to complete.

The Polos returned home with many strange and wonderful goods—porcelain, silk, ivory, and jade. Of course, some of the things they saw and tasted were impossible to bring back. Among these were the flavored ices so popular in China. Marco had written about them in his journal, though, and taken down the recipe. These ices were different from Nero's (which had been long forgotten); the Chinese added milk to their ices, making a kind of sherbet.

Most Venetians were skeptical of the Oriental world the Polos described. Who could believe in a land where people used paper money and ate in public places outside their own homes? (The Chinese had their own word for *restaurant*, but the meaning was the same.) Nobody doubted the existence of Marco's sherbet, though. Guests of the Polos could taste it for themselves. And no one cared where the recipe came from as long as Marco was willing to share it.

Marco was willing, and wealthy Venetians were delighted. The surge in trade following the Crusades had brought a return of wealth to Italy, and with wealth had come a renewed interest in fancy meals. Sherbet quickly became a valued addition to Venetian menus. It was so valued, in fact, that the nobles and merchants did not in turn share the recipe with the common people. Sherbet, they thought, was too good for ordinary folk.

They just passed it around from friend to friend and from relative to relative. In this way, the recipe spread from one Italian city to another.

Naturally, the Italian leaders had other concerns as well. Among the biggest were war and diplomacy. One way they devised to keep the peace was to arrange a marriage between members of two feuding European nobilities. A strategic wedding could sometimes prevent a war by making relatives out of rivals.

Such was the case in 1533, when Catherine de Medicis, from the Italian city of Florence, married Henri, the second son of Francis I, king of France. Both Henri and Catherine were the same age—fourteen—and they had never met before.

For Catherine, the move to France was a big step down. Italy was then the center of European culture. In Florence, Catherine was surrounded by the latest in art, fashion, and cooking. In France she would be surrounded by drafty castles and dreary meals. French food, like all the food in Northern Europe at that time, was still heavy and plain.

Catherine may have had no say about her marriage, but she did not plan to rough it in France. Maids, dressmakers, and cooks were moved along with the furniture, clothing, and dishes. Maybe Catherine couldn't dress up France by herself, but she was determined to try. No doubt the recipe for sherbet could help.

The French nobles never really liked Catherine, not even after she became queen of

France. She was too bossy for their tastes. The sherbet that she introduced to France, however, they accepted at once. Like the Italians, though, the French nobles did not share their discovery with their peasants.

The sherbet recipe that Catherine brought to France had remained largely unchanged since Marco Polo's day. The ice was still ice. The milk was still milk. The sweeteners were still honey or wine or crushed fruit. But changes were coming. Forty-one years had passed since Columbus first sailed west across the Atlantic, and the impact of his voyage on ice cream was about to be felt.

The New World—North and South America—was home to many crops, such as potatoes, corn, and tobacco, which were unknown in Europe. It was also home to the cacao bean. The Aztecs made a bitter drink with ground cacao beans called *cacahuatl*.

The Spanish explorers didn't like it plain. They drank it eagerly, though, when it was mixed with sugar. The Aztecs called the new drink *chocolatl,* and chocolate it would become.

Sugar itself was already known to Europeans. It was imported from India because the sugar cane plant could not grow in Europe. Imported sugar was rare and expensive; it was used in medicines rather than in cooking. When explorers found that sugar cane thrived on the warm islands of the Caribbean, they planted it in abundance. The resulting crops were shipped back to Europe, where people quickly developed a taste for cane sugar.

Nobody knows how much the greater availability of sugar and chocolate helped, but it was around this time that ice cream as we know it was first made. No one person has gotten the credit for inventing it. Most likely, though, the person was a professional cook who liked to experiment. The change centered on the use of ice. In the old sherbet, ice was one of the ingredients. It was mixed in a bowl with crushed fruit, juice, or milk. To make the new ice cream, milk or cream was placed in a bowl, combined with fruit, sugar, or chocolate, and *surrounded* with ice instead.

Ice cream was introduced to England during the reign of

King Charles I, who was crowned in 1625. The king loved ice cream so much, he didn't even want to share the recipe with his nobles. Supposedly he bribed his French chef to keep the recipe a secret. The English nobles were unhappy about this, but then they were unhappy with Charles about a lot of things. So were the rest of his subjects. After twenty-four years, they finally got fed up with him. In 1649, Charles I was overthrown and executed.

In France, where Louis XIV was quite secure on his throne, the secret of ice cream finally got out. In 1670, a Sicilian named Francesco Procopio opened the Cafe Procope in Paris. This was the first cafe ever opened in Paris (a city that would become famous for its cafes), and it was an immediate success. Part of that success stemmed from Procopio's decision to put ice cream on the menu. His cafe was the first place to serve ice cream to the public, and the public was very grateful.

This was the French public, of course. The English public, particularly those who had moved to America, had to wait a little longer.

The first English immigrants arrived in the British colonies with their customs, their laws, and their fashions. They did not bring any ice cream. But by the end of the 1600s, the recipe had crossed the Atlantic. The first recorded evidence of ice cream in America (and the oldest existing record of the phrase *ice cream* itself) comes from a letter written in 1700. A dinner guest of the governor of Maryland wrote that the meal had included "some fine Ice Cream which, with the Strawberries and Milk, eat most Deliciously."

Compliments like that were adding to ice cream's popularity. Recipes for it began appearing in English cookbooks. A typical recipe, which appeared in *The Art of Cookery Made Easy* (1747) by Mrs. Hanna Glasse, went as follows:

Take two Pewter Basons [sic], one larger than the other; the inward one must have closed cover, into which you are to put your Cream, and mix it with raspberries or whatever you like best, to give it a Flavour and a Colour. Sweeten it to your palate; then cover it close, and set into the larger bason [sic]. Fill it with Ice and a Handful of Salt; let it stand in this Ice three Quarters of an Hour, then uncover it, and stir the Cream well together; cover it again and let it stand Half an Hour longer, after that turn it to your Plate.

Not everyone in America wanted to make ice cream, though. Some people just wanted to eat it. By the late 1700s, several ice cream parlors had opened in New York City to serve them. This ice cream was expensive, but at least it was available to anyone who could afford it.

The growth of ice cream parlors naturally increased the demand for ice cream. In 1786, it was first manufactured commercially for sale. The manufacturers had no special equipment to help them, however. The ice cream mixture was simply put in a bowl and beaten with a spoon until it stiffened. Then the bowl was covered, placed in a bucket fiilled with ice and rock salt (ice cream cooks had learned that the salt helped freeze the mixture faster than ice alone), and shaken. People made ice cream the same way at home; they just ate it themselves instead of selling it.

One early customer of ice cream parlors was George Washington. At home in Mount Vernon, Virginia, he had two pewter ice

cream pots. Unfortunately, he was not home often during his presidency. In the summer of 1790, he lived in New York City (then the temporary capital of the United States). Mount Vernon was hundreds of miles away, and so were those ice cream pots. This was no small problem. Washington's teeth may have been wooden, but one of them was clearly a sweet tooth. He spent two hundred dollars buying ice cream that summer, certainly doing his best to make the new parlors a success.

When the presidency moved to the District of Columbia and the White House in 1800, ice cream went along. President Thomas Jefferson had learned to make ice cream years earlier while he was a diplomat of France. He continued making it when he returned home. Jefferson may have cared less about ice cream than he did about philosophy or architecture, but he certainly was serious about it. His recipe had eighteen steps—a French-style egg custard mixture had to be boiled, stirred, reheated, and generally pampered in a very particular way. After going to all that trouble, Jefferson didn't just serve the ice cream by itself. He put each scoop in a warm pastry shell. (In 1867, the chef at Delmonico's restaurant in New York covered a similar dessert with hot meringue and called it *baked Alaska*.)

The next president, James Madison, liked ice cream, too. So did his wife. Dolley Madison was a famous hostess, one who always served the finest foods. She was especially known for serving ice cream, a habit that delighted her many guests. As one of them wrote, describing a dinner she had attended:

When finally the brilliant assemblage—America's best—entered the dining room, they beheld a table set with French china and English silver, laden with good things to eat, and in the center, high on a silver platter, a large shining dome of pink ice cream.

But even Dolley Madison could not serve ice cream at every summer meal. The problem was ice—there just wasn't enough of it. There was plenty in the winter, when countless ice blocks were cut from lakes and ponds. But too many of them melted before they could be used the next summer. What

Americans needed was a better way to store them.

The Chinese had been building icehouses for two thousand years, but Americans were unfamiliar with their designs (at that point China had largely cut itself off from the outside world). European icehouses were much more primitive, but at least they were available for inspection. Americans improved on the European models in the early 1800s, developing a design with thick walls and double doors. With such protection, the ice blocks were safe from even the worst of the summer heat.

Solving the storage problem made ice a big business. In the city it was sold from ice wagons traveling up and down the streets. (In the country, people cut ice for themselves and kept it in their own icehouses.) Most of the ice was used to keep food cool in the kitchen icebox (an insulated chest with a space for ice above a storage compartment for food). Some of it, though, was used to make ice cream.

Although ice was now plentiful, making ice cream remained a difficult task. The favored *pot freezer* method wasn't much fun. First the ice cream mixture was put in a bowl inside a bucket or canister lined with ice and salt. That was the simple part. Then the whole thing had to be shaken while the ice cream mixture was stirred. That was the part that took energy and muscle. It also raised a lot of questions. Was it better to shake the bucket up and down or from side to side? Or both? How hard should it be shaken? Did it hurt to peek at the ice cream when your arms got tired?

Many of the difficulties with the pot freezer method were alleviated when Nancy Johnson invented the hand-cranked ice cream freezer in 1846. It featured a metal pail sitting in a wooden bucket. The ice cream mixture was put in the pail. Crushed ice and rock salt were put in the space between the pail and the bucket. A crank turned a paddle inside the pail, which, in turn, stirred the ice cream evenly as it froze. People still had to turn the crank, and that still took muscles, but at least they didn't have to shake the mixture and could turn it sitting down.

Nobody knows why Nancy Johnson failed to patent her invention. The fact remains that she didn't. On May 30, 1848, William G. Young, a man who had no part in creating the freezer, registered it with the Patent Office. Giving credit where credit was due, he called his product the "Johnson Patent Ice Cream Freezer." But credit was all he shared with Nancy Johnson. Young kept the profits for himself.

There were a lot of profits to make. Thousands of people happily bought the machine to use at home. Ice cream making became something of a ritual, a distinct part of a picnic or family party. Children usually took turns with the crank, but there was never a shortage of helpers. After all, whoever helped with the cranking got to lick the paddle clean later.

All that cranking was making ice cream an increasingly common treat. And the more common it became, the more likely people were to experiment with it. When ice cream itself had been a novelty, nobody had thought of combining it with things other than fruit and chocolate flavorings. Now the novelty was wearing off.

One promising place for an experiment was the local soda fountain. The first one had opened in a Philadelphia drugstore in 1825. With its gleaming counters and sparkling glasses, it soon had many imitators. As the name suggests, soda fountains sold soda. (The early flavors included root beer, ginger, lemon, cherry, and kola.) Soda fountains sold ice cream, too. Some customers came in for one, some for the other, and a few came in

for both. But nobody thought of putting them together.

When the idea finally occurred to Robert M. Green, it was only in desperation. Green sold sodas at Philadelphia's Franklin Institute during its fiftieth birthday celebration in 1874. Among his offerings was a soda mixed with ordinary cream. One day, though, business was better than expected, and Green ran out of cream. Unwilling to turn away customers, he began adding vanilla ice cream (which he sold separately) to the soda instead. It wasn't a perfect substitute, but Green hoped nobody would notice. He didn't get his wish. Luckily for him, everybody noticed. They all loved the new concoction.

Mixing ice cream and soda was only the beginning. Toppings—syrups, marshmallow, nuts, whipped cream, candy, and fruit—were next. They appeared in the Midwest during the 1890s, and several places claim credit for presenting them first. Paul Dickson, in *The Great American Ice Cream Book,* cites the two following stories as the likeliest contenders for the honor.

In Evanston, Illinois, ice cream sodas were big sellers, even on Sundays. This troubled the town leaders, who thought Sundays should be reserved for more religious concerns. These leaders did more than grumble among themselves; they passed a local law that made it illegal to make ice cream sodas on Sundays. Naturally, this upset the soda fountain owners. They had been doing a good business in Sunday sodas. Although they reluctantly obeyed the new law, they also worked their way around it. Instead of making sodas on Sunday, they began to put

SODA FOUNTAIN ~ 1876

toppings on ice cream and to sell that instead. These *sundays*, as they were soon called, were as popular as the sodas had ever been. (A *sunday* became a *sundae* when people complained that the name itself was disrespectful to the Sabbath.)

The tale was different at Ed Berner's soda fountain in Two Rivers, Wisconsin. There a boy named George Hallauer simply asked

Berner to pour chocolate syrup over his dish of ice cream. Berner was skeptical, but George insisted. The boy was so pleased with the result that Berner later tried the concotion himself. He soon added it to his menu, and the news traveled fast. At a soda fountain

nearby, the customers began demanding ice cream with syrup, too. The owner, George Giffy, was afraid he would lose money on the new dish (it cost a nickel, just like plain ice cream) so he served it only on Sundays. The name followed from that. When *sundays* proved to be profitable, Giffy changed the name to *sundaes* because he was now serving them every day of the week.

Whichever story came first, the result was the same—ice cream sales climbed rapidly. Supply was able to keep pace with demand because an ice cream industry had developed. Commercial production had entered a new age in 1851 when Jacob Fussell built the first ice cream factory. Fussell was a Baltimore milk dealer who had to estimate how much milk and cream he should order from surrounding farms. Sometimes he guessed wrong and found himself stuck with a lot of extra cream. When the cream went sour on him, his profits soured, too. Simply to get rid of the extra cream, Fussell started turning it into ice cream. He sold his ice cream for 25 cents a quart—less than half of what smaller ice cream makers charged.

Sales were great. Fussell did so well selling ice cream (even after he raised his prices) that he gave up the milk business altogether. In the following years he opened factories in six more cities. Although these factories were devoted to ice cream making, they still used hand-crank machines at first. Other people expanded the industry even further. By 1900, Americans were happily eating five million gallons of ice cream a year.

Many of these people went to the 1904 World's Fair in St. Louis. The fair was supposed to be celebrating the one hundredth anniversary of the Louisiana Purchase. It found time and space to celebrate a lot of other things, too. The exhibitions featured the scientific wonders of the era—an early radio, telephone switchboards, silent movies, and airplanes (which had first been flown only the year before).

ICE CREAM

GET YOUR ZALABIAS

All the walking around in the hot summer was great for ice cream sales. The vendors were surrounded by crowds; they couldn't scoop the ice cream up fast enough. One of them was so busy, he ran out of paper dishes. At the booth next door, Ernest Hamwi was selling a kind of thin waffle called a *zalabia*. Thinking fast, Hamwi took a hot zalabia and rolled it into a cone. He then offered it to the ice cream vendor as a substitute for the dish. The vendor decided to try it. He put a scoop of ice cream in the cone—and sold it at once. The cones were an instant success. Dozens of vendors were serving them before the fair ended. (Paul Dickson credits an Italian named Italo Marchiony for actually inventing the cone because he patented a pastry cup in 1896. The cone remained unknown to the public, though, until the 1904 World's Fair.)

Ice cream's popularity kept growing as more and more ways to eat it appeared. The five million gallons a year consumed in 1900 became thirty million gallons in 1909. By

1919, Americans were spooning through 150 million gallons a year. This dramatic increase was due partly to the sharp rise in the population (seventeen million immigrants entered the country between 1900 and 1920) and partly to improved machinery. With the help of steam power and then electricity, commercially made ice cream finally said farewell to the hand-crank era.

But ice cream enthusiasts could look forward to more advances. In 1919, Christian Nelson, an Iowa candy store owner, watched one of his customers struggle with a decision. The boy was trying to decide how to spend his nickel. Should it go for ice cream or a chocolate bar? This struggle gave Nelson an idea. No one should be forced to make such a choice, he thought. Why not create an ice cream bar covered with a chocolate shell? The shell would taste good, and it would be an edible holder for the ice cream besides.

Nelson called his discovery the I-Scream Bar. To market it, he became partners with an ice cream company worker named Russell

Stover. Stover suggested a new name for the bar, and in 1921, the Eskimo Pie first appeared. A year later, they were selling at the incredible rate of one million bars a day.

More variations were on the way. Soft ice cream appeared in the 1920s, pumped out of a machine like thick toothpaste. In the next few years, the Dixie Cup (ice cream in a small cardboard cup) and the ice cream sandwich (notably the San Francisco It's It bar, which was made with oatmeal cookies) appeared. Meanwhile Harry Burt, owner of an Ohio ice cream parlor, put the first chocolate-covered ice cream bar on a stick (mostly because his own experiments with chocolate coverings had been so messy). Burt called his creation the Good Humor Ice Cream Sucker. Although he died in 1926, his business prospered. The Good Humor Man, wearing his white uniform and driving his white truck, was soon a familiar figure at the beach and the park.

The humble stick soon found another home as well. In early 1923, Frank Epperson, a California lemonade maker, came east to

visit friends in New Jersey. While there, he made up a special batch of lemonade. Epperson stirred a glass of the lemonade with a spoon and left it overnight on a windowsill. The lemonade froze around the spoon in the cold weather. Epperson found it there the next morning. He warmed the glass under water, and when it came off, he was left holding the frozen juice by the spoon. Epperson looked hard at his creation—and then he made the most of it. In 1924, he patented the Epsicle (later renamed the Popsicle), which brought ice cream back to its roots as a water ice.

The Depression of 1929 brought the

growth of American business to a harsh stop. One quarter of the work force became unemployed, and ice cream was not high on the list of anyone's priorities. But even as ice cream sales suffered, the image of ice cream never looked better. It was a featured prop in movies and a popular lyric in songs. Ice cream had become as American as apple pie and the two were often served together.

Unlike apple pie, though, ice cream had to be kept frozen for storage. In most homes there was not yet a place to do this. The old iceboxes kept foods cool, but ice cream would have slowly melted all over the bottom.

A colder storage space was needed. Since the early 1800s, scientists had been studying the principles of mechanical refrigeration. They had found that certain liquids, like ether and ammonia, radiated great cold when vaporized under pressure. This principle had led to the creation of the refrigerated railroad car half a century later. People had no room in their homes for railroad cars, so they had to wait longer. The first home refrigerators appeared around 1920. They were the right size, but like many new products, they were too expensive for most people. Further improvements and increased production soon brought down the price. By the 1930s, the home refrigerator, complete with a small freezer compartment big enough for ice cream, was a common household appliance.

Many different kinds of ice cream could be kept in that freezer. A new chain of restaurants, Howard Johnson's, advertised twenty-eight flavors to choose from. The Baskin-Robbins ice cream stores would later offer thirty-one flavors from a revolving storehouse of hundreds. Some of the flavors on record are more daring than tasty. They have ranged from brassicaceous beer (root beer and horseradish) to chile con carne.

The increase in flavors after World War II was more than matched by an increase in mass production. Until the 1920s, a commercial machine made one batch of ice cream at a time. (Each batch was big, but the process

Our World Famous Flavors

ITALIAN MEATBALL	HUMPBACK WHALE
INDIGESTION	LEFT OVER LIVER & ONIONS
OLD GALOSHES	COLD GRAVY
TRENCH MOUTH	OVEN CLEANER
OLD LOUISIANA SWAMP	SPARKLING SLUDGE
MR. KLEAN	TWITCH
OLD FASHIONED RUST	OUR FAMOUS BLUE MOLD
FORGOTTEN CHEESE	TANGY OLD SNEAKER
OCTOPUS	SLOW BURNING TIRE
VANILLA	OINTMINT
TODAY'S SPECIAL COCOON	YESTERDAY'S SPECIAL OLD BROOM CLOSET

for producing it was similar to making ice cream at home.) If a company wanted to make more batches, they bought more machines. The development of the continuous freezer by Clarence Vogt changed the process. With his machine, an ice cream mixture was put in at one end and ice cream itself came out the other. Just one of his freezers could make a lot more ice cream much faster than the older machines.

This assembly-line approach is still used today. First, the basic mixture is sterilized with heat to kill any harmful bacteria (a process invented by Louis Pasteur in 1895). Ice cream mixtures are pasteurized at 155 degrees Fahrenheit (68 degrees centigrade) for thirty minutes. Then the mixture is homogenized (blended together for a more even consistency), cooled, and shot through a refrigerated tube (a descendant of Vogt's continuous freezer) in seconds. When it comes out, the ice cream is partially frozen. Fruits, nuts, or liquid flavorings are then added. Afterward, the ice cream is put in a cold room to freeze completely. When the ice cream is ready, it is delivered to stores in refrigerated trucks.

Commercial ice cream recipes have changed along with the technology. Since the soda fountains and ice cream parlors of the past used up their ice cream in a few days, their suppliers simply relied on fresh ingredients to make it. Most of today's ice cream, headed for the supermarket, is designed to last for weeks or months. Many fresh ingredients would spoil in that time. To extend modern ice cream's shelf life—and to save money—cream, sugar, and eggs have been at least partially replaced by dry milk, corn sweetener, powdered eggs, stabilizers, and emulsifiers. (The stabilizers—gelatin or gum—give ice cream a smooth texture that prevents grainy ice crystals from forming. The emulsifiers make the ice cream more whippable.) Other chemicals provide texture and artificial flavor. Modern ice cream is also heavily pumped up with air. All ice cream has some of this *overrun,* but some brands overdo it. And while the federal government has set guidelines for the ingredients ice cream must contain, the guidelines leave a lot of loopholes for manufacturers.

Partly in response to this drop in quality, homemade ice cream parlors have been making a comeback. At one of them in Somerville, Massachusetts, Steve Herrell created an innovation called the Mix-in in 1973. At the customer's request, crushed cookies or pieces of candy were mixed into (not simply sprinkled on top of) a scoop of ice cream. The Mix-in has been a feature of most ice cream parlors ever since.

Anyone can make ice cream in much the same way these new stores do. All you need is the ingredients, chopped ice and rock salt, and an ice cream maker—either  a hand-crank or motorized model. A good recipe for vanilla ice cream (half of all the ice cream made in the United States is still good old vanilla) is the following:

Mix together 1 quart of light cream, 3 cups of sugar, and 3 teaspoons of vanilla extract. Heat the mixture in a double boiler until the cream is bubbling around the edges. Let the mixture cool, and then add 2 more quarts of light cream. Put the mixture in your ice cream maker, packing in the ice and salt according to the directions. If you wish, add other ingredients—chocolate chips, raisins, nuts, berries—as the mixture is churning away (the ice cream maker will do the work of mixing them in for you).

Whether eaten in new or traditional ways, ice cream is taking a greater licking than ever before. Ice cream consumption in the United States has risen to 800 million gallons a year. That works out to fifteen quarts each for the average American. Of course, that counts the average American who prefers frozen custard (ice cream with more eggs added), gelato (smooth, strongly flavored ice cream with less milk fat), ice milk (ice cream with about half the milk fat content), soft ice cream (ice milk

that was not frozen hard), sherbet (a flavored ice with a small milk fat content), and sorbet (like sherbet without the milk fat).

Nero, Marco Polo, and Charles I of England all would probably enjoy these products, though they might prefer not to share them with everyone else. Fortunately, there's plenty of ice cream to go around now, so one thing is certain: Whatever changes are introduced to ice cream in the future, the rest of us will get to enjoy them, too.

INDEX